if i crossed the road

written and illustrated by Stephen Kroninger

AN ANNE SCHWARTZ BOOK

ATHENEUM BOOKS FOR YOUNG READERS

**The art for this book consists of collage
created from magazine photographs and cut paper.**

Atheneum Books for Young Readers
An imprint of Simon & Schuster Children's Publishing Division
1230 Avenue of the Americas
New York, New York 10020

Book design by Angela Carlino
The text of this book is set in American Typewriter Bold.

First Edition
Printed in Singapore
10 9 8 7 6 5 4 3 2

Library of Congress Cataloging-in-Publication Data
Kroninger, Stephen.
If I crossed the road / Stephen Kroninger.—1st ed.
p.   cm.
"An Anne Schwartz book."
Summary: A young boy imagines the fantastic things that might await him,
if only his mother would let him cross the road.
ISBN 0-689-81190-X
[1. Imagination—Fiction. 2. Mother and child—Fiction.] I. Title.
PZ7.K9228If   1997
[E]—DC21
96-49450

For Aviva

My mom says I'm too little
to cross the road by myself.

But I'm not too little
to **THINK** about it.
If I could cross the road . . .

I'd ride my bike all
the way to the park.

I'd play ball!

Then I'd visit my grandpa.

I'd go fishing.

Maybe I'd even look
for a new pet.

I'd see the city.
And when I got
bored,

I'd go somewhere . . .

to get ice cream.

I'd do all kinds of stuff if I could cross the road.

But what I'd MOST like to do . . .

is visit my best friend.